Two Birthdays
for Beth

by
Gay Lynn Cronin

Perspectives Press
Indianapolis, Indiana

Illustrated by Joanne Bowring

Perspectives Press
P.O. Box 90318
Indianapolis, IN 46290-0318
U.S.A.

Manufactured in the United States of America
ISBN 0-944934-13-7

Library of Congress Cataloging-in-Publication Data

Cronin, Gay Lynn, 1962-
    Two birthdays for Beth / by Gay Lynn Cronin ; illustrated by Joanne Bowring.
        p.   cm.
    Summary: After waiting for months for a second birthday celebration because she is adopted, a young girl is initially disappointed--until she realizes how lucky she is.
    ISBN 0-944934-13-7
    [1. Adoption--Fiction. 2. Birthdays--Fiction. 3. Mothers and daughters--Fiction.] I. Bowring, Joanne, ill. II. Title.
PZ7.C8814Tw   1995
[Fic]--dc20   94-39797
                                                          CIP
                                                          AC

Beth snuggled onto Mom's lap. Together they rocked back and forth, back and forth. She listened as Mom told Beth's very own adoption story.

"You came from your birth mother's body and my heart. On June first you became my little girl. We ate chocolate cake with pink icing. Up to the ceiling we stacked your presents," Mom said.

"Wow! Presents?
Like a birthday party?" Beth asked.

Mom nodded.

After Mom left, Beth grabbed her doll, Emily.

"Yippie! Two birthdays!' Beth told Emily. Emily smiled back at Beth.

"On June first I'll get chocolate cake with pink icing and oodles of presents. Maybe I'll get another doll to be your friend."

Beth thought she saw Emily smile wider.

The next day Beth asked, "Is it June yet?'

"Not yet," said Mom. "It's March.

When days get warm, June will come."

Beth wished and waited.

One sunny morning she swung on her swing without her blue jacket.

It must be June now.

"Is it June yet?" Beth asked.

"Not yet," said Grandpa. "It's April.
When flowers bloom, June will come."

Finally the tulips bloomed
red, yellow, and pink,
like a rainbow.

"It must be June now."

"Not yet," said Beth's teacher. "It's May.
When school's done, June will come."

Beth wished and waited. Finally school ended.

"Is it June yet?"

"Tomorrow," Mom said.

Tomorrow!

On June first, Beth grabbed Emily, ran
downstairs and flung open the refrigerator door.

She saw tomatoes and potatoes.

No chocolate cake.

There were purple grapes
and lemon crepes.

No chocolate cake.

She found sandwich spread
and whole wheat bread.

No chocolate cake.

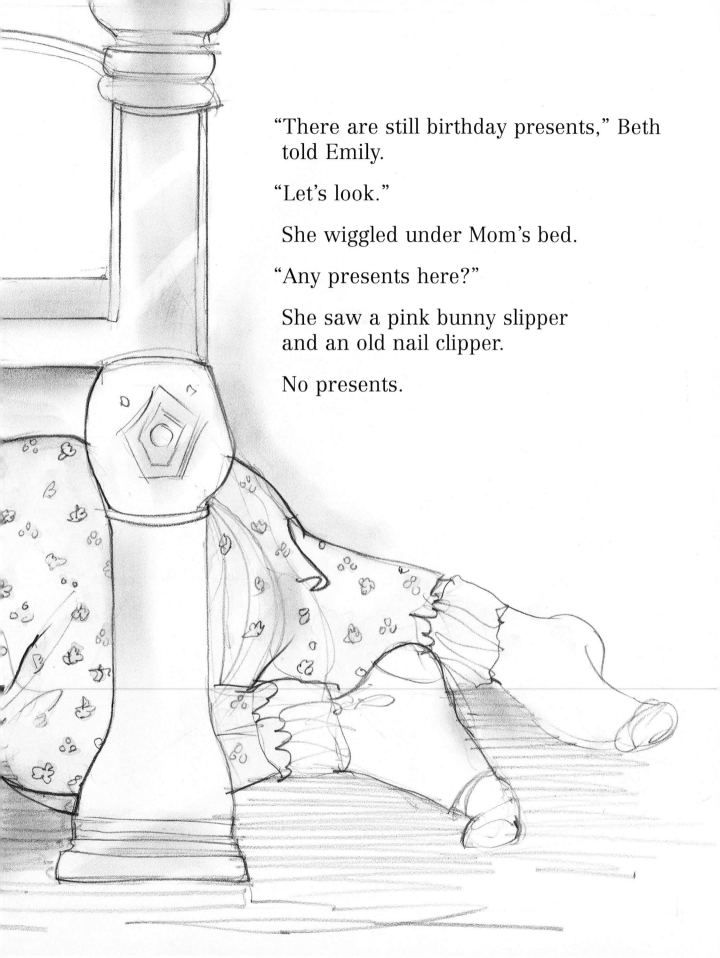

"There are still birthday presents," Beth told Emily.

"Let's look."

She wiggled under Mom's bed.

"Any presents here?"

She saw a pink bunny slipper and an old nail clipper.

No presents.

Beth climbed up to the tip-top closet shelf.

She found furry winter boots
and a horn that toots.

No presents.

"Uh-oh."

C-R-A-S-H!

Beth tumbled smack into the laundry basket.
It felt like a fluffy cloud. Meanwhile, boxes fell
everywhere!

Little boxes,

big boxes,

long boxes,

short boxes

toppled.

But no birthday presents fell. Even Emily
looked worried.

Mom came running. "What happened?"

"You forgot my birthday. There's no chocolate
cake and no presents."

Mom frowned. "Your birthday is in January."

Beth hugged Emily. "But I'm adopted.
I get *two* birthdays!"

"Everyone has only one birthday," Mom said.

"No birthday presents today?"

Mom shook her head.

"No chocolate cake today?"

Mom shook her head.

Beth climbed onto Mom's lap.

"When is my *one* birthday?"

"Past summer days
when sunshine plays…"

"Then?" Beth asked.

"Not yet…

"Past leaves that swirl
their autumn twirl."

"Then?" Beth asked.

"Not yet…

"Past a cold night
with snowflakes white."

Beth climbed down.

"It's forever," she said with a frown.

Even Emily looked sad.

"I wished and waited a long time for you," Mom said. "Now we're a family."

"I'd like to give you chocolate cake and presents every day, but I can't," Mom said. "Birthdays only come once a year."

Beth plopped onto the floor.

"Being adopted is different, so I thought it meant two birthdays."

Mom kissed her forehead.

"Adoption is different, but the love is the same. I don't love you because you're adopted. I love you because you're Beth. And I think Beth is absolutely wonderful, don't you?"

Beth looked up at Mom.

She remembered her very own adoption story.

Then Beth smiled. She had an idea.

"Wait here," Beth said.

In her room, Beth folded a piece of red paper.

She colored and clipped,
snapped and snipped,
drew and dipped.

Grabbing a box, she stuck her present inside.

"For me?" Mom asked.

Beth nodded.

Mom opened the box. She lifted out the folded red heart.

"Open it up…See?"

"This side is you. This side is me.
Together we make a heart.
Together we make a family. Every day.
That's what being adopted means," Beth said.

She hugged Mom.

"Please let *me* tell the story."

She snuggled onto Mom's lap. Together they rocked back and forth, back and forth.

Beth told her very own adoption story.

Mom held the red paper heart against her own heart.

And Emily just smiled.

About the author

Gay Lynn Cronin is a free-lance writer and newsletter editor. She writes frequently about parenting and health issues. The newsletter *Care & Courage* provides information and objective support for single mothers and women experiencing unplanned pregnancies.

Gay Lynn and her husband, John, reside in suburban Chicago and are parents of two young daughters. Although her daughter's question of when her birthday would arrive sparked *Two Birthdays for Beth,* Gay Lynn's own experience as an adoptee allowed her to write it.

About the illustrator

Joanne Bowring has been an artist and illustrator for 20 years. She illustrates middle school textbooks and children's books, including self publishing *Mr. Fuzzy H.U.G.S.* along with the author. She has illustrated several books for Perspectives Press, including *Real For Sure Sister, Where the Sun Kisses the Sea,* and *Let Me Explain.*

Joanne enjoys volunteering for children in the local grade school in a program to get their own books and poetry published. Joanne lives in Wauwatosa, Wisconsin, with her husband, Doug, and children, Mary and Tim.

About the publisher

Since 1982 Perspectives Press has focused on infertility, adoption, and related reproductive health and child welfare issues. Our purpose is to promote understanding of these issues and to educate and sensitize those personally experiencing these life situations, the professionals who work in these fields, and the public at large. In addition to this book, our current titles include eight books for adults and the following books for children:

Our Baby: A Birth and Adoption Story

The Mulberry Bird: Story of an Adoption

Real for Sure Sister

Filling in the Blanks: A Guided Look at Growing Up Adopted

Where the Sun Kisses the Sea

William Is My Brother

Lucy's Feet

Let Me Explain: A Story about Donor Insemination

If you feel you may have a book for our audience, contact us with stamped self addressed envelope for a copy of our catalog and writer's guidelines.

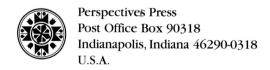

Perspectives Press
Post Office Box 90318
Indianapolis, Indiana 46290-0318
U.S.A.